YOU DO UNDERSTAND

YOU DO UNDERSTAND
ANDREJ BLATNIK
translated by Tamara M. Soban

Dalkey Archive Press
Champaign & London

The translator would like to thank Dean DeVos for his invaluable editorial input

Originally published in Slovenian as *Saj razumeš?* by LUD Literatura, 2009
Copyright © 2009 by Andrej Blatnik
Translation copyright © 2010 by Tamara M. Soban
First edition, 2010

Library of Congress Cataloging-in-Publication Data

Blatnik, Andrej.
[Saj razumeš. English]
You do understand / Andrej Blatnik ; translated by Tamara M. Soban. -- 1st ed.
p. cm.
Originally published in Slovenian as Saj razumeš? in 2009.
ISBN 978-1-56478-599-2 (pbk. : alk. paper)
1. Blatnik, Andrej--Translations into English. 2. Interpersonal relations--Fiction.
3. Short stories, Slovenian--Translations into English. I. Soban, Tamara. II. Title.
PG1919.12.L38S3513 2010
891.8'435--dc22
                                                2010011886

Partially funded by the University of Illinois at Urbana-Champaign
and by a grant from the Illinois Arts Council, a state agency

This work has been published with the financial support of the Trubar Foundation,
located at the Slovene Writers' Association, Ljubljana, Slovenia

This translation has been financially supported by the Slovenian Book Agency

The Slovenian Literature Series is made possible
by support from the Slovenian Book Agency

www.dalkeyarchive.com

Cover: design and composition by Danielle Dutton, illustration by Nicholas Motte
Printed on permanent/durable acid-free paper
and bound in the United States of America

I thought
that pain meant
I was not loved.
It meant I loved.

—Louise Glück, "First Memory"

FEW WORDS

"Do you believe in a tomorrow together?"

"First I'd like to believe tonight really happened."

SAVE YOUR KISSES FOR ME

Sometimes the curtain doesn't even rise, he thought, a moment before stepping onto the stage. And sometimes it rises, but there's not a single girl out there and you don't even have to go up to the mike. And sometimes they start booing before you even start singing and then it's like you've won the race by default, you don't even have to show how much you don't know, you just spread your arms and walk away. But sometimes, sometimes there's a lot of them on the other side, clapping and cheering enthusiastically as though they can't wait for you to start singing off-key, and that's when you're in trouble, that's when you have to take your guitar and sing the way that you can't, that's when you can't take a step back and say "I knew it," to yourself and the world. It can't be one of those nights that some girl shows up, can it?

WAS I?

I can't remember a thing. I went out someplace with my girlfriends from school in the evening, and then we went to another place, and then another, I can't remember, and then those guys showed up. Yeah, we messed around a bit, but no heavy stuff. They kept buying us drinks, but I can't remember what I had. I remember me and him talking in the hallway outside the restrooms. I remember we waved, he to his gang, me to mine. I remember he had a motorcycle, he fastened a helmet on for me. His helmet. It was too large for me but it smelled good. The rest of the guys smelled like boys, but he smelled—different. Grown up.

My girlfriends asked me: Were you drunk? Was he gentle? Did your mom see him? Did he give you his number? I can't remember. I can't remember anything except that smell in his helmet.

AND SINCE I COULDN'T SLEEP

I've left. I know I have to leave a note. I know it's not right for a girl to walk out like this after you've taken her to dinner, or rather, after you've been wining and dining her for three months, virtually every night, and after she's said, for the first time, after your nearly one hundred dinners together, that yes, tonight she would like that nightcap. I know it's hard to wake up and find an empty bed when the night before you were so sure it wouldn't be empty in the morning, to wake up to an empty apartment when you thought it wouldn't have to be empty anymore. But I had to leave, I couldn't sleep, you do understand, don't you.

What can I say? That it was a lovely evening? You know that already. I always told you so. It was always lovely. That I couldn't stay? You know that too. You can see I'm gone. All those dinners—I wasn't really that hungry, you know. But it was nice afterward, when they'd cleared away the dishes and we just sat there, chatting. I liked the way you always slowly shook your head no when I offered to pay the bill. I could have paid, you know, almost every time, not just once, but I liked your slow head shake. It made your hair undulate.

Yes, I know we'd had too much to eat already and it was time to move on to other things. That's why I said we could go to your place. But the moment we walked in through your door I knew we shouldn't have. All that stuff in your apartment! There was no room for me. While we were out eating it was less—personal. Here, though—I don't know, maybe we should've gone to a hotel, maybe that would have worked. Like in a restaurant, you come and you go. This, though, was your home. All those things on the walls, objects you and your wife had brought back from trips. You even showed me your kids' room. Yes, that was a mistake, as I'm sure you realize. I know they're grown up and on their own. But they still have a room at your place. They could come back, anytime. And what would I do then?

I felt bad when you cried. I wish I could've been more of a comfort to you, but I couldn't. Yes, I know you care about me. I care about you, too. And I'm really sorry, because you're a nice guy. Other guys wouldn't have made up a bed for me in the living room. But I really couldn't. Sleep. Too many things. Those books that can't really belong to you. That music you never listen to. Too much for me, sorry.

You know something? I'm very full. I don't think I'll be able to eat anymore, at least not for a while. And what else is there for us to do? You're not offended, are you? You do understand, don't you?

MELTING POINT

Pressing the stop button on the tape recorder, she was nervous. Legend had it that he'd slept with every woman who attended his famous pottery class, even those who didn't care for men, even those who didn't care for anyone. What would happen now that they'd done the interview? How would he make his move? His swelling ceramics bulged toward her, she felt she couldn't think straight with all those exposed, polished curves around. Legend had it that she'd never slept with anyone, not even the people who never gave interviews to anyone, the people who never gave interviews to anyone but her.

Smiling, he said: "I really enjoy listening to you, you know."

Aha, here we go. "You—you listen to the radio?"

"It's quite lonesome here in the studio, for the most part—" *Getting personal.*

"—and I'm always so happy when I can fill the room with such a sensuous voice . . . like yours." *Do you really think I'm as easy as all the others?*

"The thing is, I'm rather lonely." *Sure, and I really feel for you, shithead.*

"I've had a lot of women, you know—" *I know, I know, they all know.*

"—but none of them turned out to be the right one." *Now he's going to say, "Until I met you!"*

"You're just the opposite, I hear. There haven't been many—"

Haven't been many? Who on earth could he have heard about?

"—so I'm sure that when you find one, it'll be the right one for you."

Now he's going to say, "Are you sure it isn't me?"

"Well, it was nice of you to come by. See you around. Good-bye."

She stood in the street, listening to the recording, smart questions, evasive answers, and couldn't believe it.

That was it? Just that?

She went back and said:

"I'm sorry. Something went wrong. The tape is blank. We'll have to give it another try."

QED

"So you're saying you've traveled a lot," says the woman I met yesterday, three hours and quite a few drinks ago.

"A lot," I say. *I have, actually.*

"You must be used to everything then, nothing can come as a surprise anymore," she says.

"Nothing whatsoever," I say securely, "I'm used to absolutely everything." *Okay, more or less.*

"So you're saying that," she says, "if that kid by the bar stripped, if she dropped all her clothes on the floor, that would be something totally ordinary for you, something you've seen hundreds of times?"

I look at the kid. She's cute all right, not wearing much, but too drunk to do much of anything, she can barely hold on to the bar. *The only trick that girl's likely to pull is falling over.*

"Oh, that would just break me up," I say superciliously. "Because, you know, there are limits, I'm a decent man, there are things I can't stand, this rampant nudity everywhere, it's really disgusting—" *I'm really getting into the part now, just a little further and I'll end up believing it myself.*

"Oh come on," she says. "It's just skin, it's no big deal. Look."

She pulls up her shirt. *She has nothing underneath it, nothing but—*

I can't look, though it's a pleasant sight, but—*everyone can see! Is she nuts? How can they just carry on drinking, how can the guy behind the bar go on rinsing out glasses while this woman here . . . Is this normal for them? Does she do this regularly? With a different guy every time?*

She gives a mock smile, only turning up the corners of her mouth.

When I calm down a little, when my eyes stop flitting all over the place and I stop blushing, she gives me a penetrating look: "So, of all the places you've visited, which was your favorite?"

AN ALMOST PERFECT EVENING

You know I'm well brought-up—I take tea at five and I abhor infanticide. But I'd love to see you just once pleading for a drink outside some working-class joint, begging incoherently for spare change from discomfited housewives, pulling some man on top of you in a roadside ditch. You know I do what's expected of me—I tip waiters, I don't litter. But I'd love to see you just once dribbling your drink down your chin as you take your glass away from your mouth, soiling the front of your dress, stumbling on your way to the bathroom, forgetting to button up when you come back, falling, trying in vain to fit your arm into the sleeve of your coat, begging passersby to give you a lift home though you can't quite recall where that is at the moment. You know I know what's right and proper. But I still suffer when I see you go on carefully fixing your lipstick, adjusting your hemline to a strategic length, smiling sweetly and insisting that you'd like to pay for once, it's really your turn this time. And I order one drink after another, knocking them back desperately, the receipts piling up in front of me, and tell myself, my inner voice slurring the words more and more: "I'm miserable, I *truly* am miserable."

VOYEUR

Everything is in place, the ashtray virtually brimming over, the tablecloth splattered red, the glasses mottled, it's the dead of night, nobody's listening when she says: No, not even once with a man she liked. Touched, somebody smiles: What an appealing story!

DO IT QUICKLY, SHE SAID,

and I felt like things were getting out of hand, are you okay? I asked, immediately angry at myself, she must've heard the tremor in my voice, she must've thought I couldn't keep it up, we must be almost there by now, even though I'm sure it'll still be too soon, I can't feel a thing, she said, are you done? I don't think I am, I thought, but I'm not about to go into that now, I should know, I guess, I can't tell her I don't know, not now, this is all too bizarre already, how did I get myself into this, all I wanted was to go home, oh right, I am at home, except that it's not the way it usually is, usually I turn on the DVD player, the buttons on the remote obey me, forward and back, slowly, frame by frame, but this here—aren't you done yet? she asked, could we do it another way? because you know this isn't exactly—well, I don't want to go into that now, it's taking too long as it is, but what the hell, I should've thought of that sooner,

.

shouldn't I, I won't bust your balls anymore, just get on with it, are you going to take much longer, because I've got to say it's much quicker with other guys, not that I've had that many, but I still think this is taking far longer than the average, I don't know, maybe it's something to do with your age—could you please just shut up for a little while please, I thought, it would be over by now and I could leave, oh right, I can't leave, it's my apartment, but I hope you'll leave, quickly, though if I remember correctly I told you you could stay as long as you liked, ohmygod, you didn't take that seriously did you, because this could last a long time, you're not staying are you, you're going, right, because if you stay, everything will have to change, everything will have to become different if you stay, it could go on forever—I'd like to get out of here before I die of old age, you know, I can't stay long, she said, I'd like to leave, come on, do it quickly, I'll wait, I can do that much, but don't take forever, I couldn't handle that, I just want to leave, just get it over with.

MISUNDERSTANDING

"You're even more beautiful when you come," he said.
How would you know? she thought.

ONE

Lying in the darkness of my room, I feel the animal lick my hand, which, leaving the day behind, has curled in on itself, a shriveled coil. The animal radiates a feverish shimmer; its wet tongue flicking over my parched skin sends sparks flying. Because I can't name the animal, I think: I've made this animal up. *I believe* I've made it up, not that this makes any difference: *It is here*. It lies, softly panting, on my bed, content, and I feel that its panting is a message: Yeah, that's right, you made me up. Made me up very well indeed, down to the last detail, down to this hunger boring a hole in my insides. Please go on imagining me, otherwise I won't be able to lunge at you and crush your windpipe when I can't bear it anymore.

I think I should stop thinking about it, if I've really made it up, if it isn't actually real. Like this room, which seems to be a room, although I know that in reality I'm in the womb of a body I don't recognize. But as usual, the worst-case scenario is that all apparent contrast is just sameness, reflected back as though in a mirror: What if the animal is also thinking me? Then we're both finished, no matter which one of us makes the first move. This is why I lie in a room that is not a room, while the animal, nervous with hunger, licks my hand.

SAY THAT

Say that you're kissing a strange girl. Yes, things like that
do happen. Say that you'd gone to a bar, you'd drunk
even more than usual, say that you hadn't gone along
with your colleagues this time, remembering your wife
sneering as you picked up your briefcase: "Do all these
meetings have to end up in a strip joint? Couldn't you
go, I don't know, pick up used needles down by the
train station instead?" So you'd thought of her and told
your colleagues you wouldn't be coming with them today, and then you'd ended up in this bar. And when this
girl joined you at your table because all the other seats
were taken, it didn't feel wrong. And when you paid
for the drinks and she thanked you and lightly touched
your arm, it didn't feel wrong. And when you leaned
close to her and spoke into her ear because it was getting noisier and noisier and her skin was nearer and
nearer, it didn't feel wrong. You thought: If you look

down into an abyss, there's a force that pulls you in, you can't help it, there's nothing wrong with that. But when you caressed her knee, sort of inadvertently, and then a bit more and a bit higher, you felt that there might be something there, something possibly slightly wrong. That things might not be what they seem.

Sure, you'd read that funny dating-advice book. *How can you tell the gender of your date in advance? In men, the ring finger is longer than the index finger, the knuckles are hairy, the Adam's apple is prominent, the shoulders are broader than the hips.* That sort of thing. But the bar is dark. Too dark. And you don't know if perhaps something might be terribly wrong.

These things happen, things that are terribly wrong. Your wife doesn't like you going to strip clubs, you think. But there, in a strip club, things are clear. What you see is what you get. Everything's in plain sight. You're told the prices at the bar. But what about now? What now? You reach for your cell phone. No, your colleagues won't give you advice, they'll laugh at you, they'll say: "Go for it, go the whole nine yards. If you can't tell the difference it doesn't matter anyway." But it does matter. There is definitely a difference. Who can you call? What would your wife say if you called and said, "I'm not at a strip club, and I'm not picking up used needles either, I'm kissing someone and I'm not sure—"

No, this isn't acceptable. That's why the warm lips moving up your neck fill you with dread: It's nearly closing time, and maybe even then they won't turn up the lights, maybe you'll both just rise to leave and probably that's when that little question will be posed: "Coming with me?" What do you say then? There are, as always, two options. But which one's the right one? You wish you were in a strip club with your friends, you'd know what to say, you'd say, "Check, please!" and leave, everything would be all right. When they asked you if you were coming along, you should have said yes. Soon now the same question might get asked. And what are you going to say?

SEPARATION

It's odd to wake up in a strange apartment. You look at the woman lying next to you. How did you get here? You can't strike up a conversation with a woman reading Coelho on the train, really. And yet, it happens. Now you're here. She's asleep. You listen: She's still breathing. It would be awful if she wasn't. Who would you call? How would you explain? As it is, everything can be repaired. On the floor, the remnants of last night, leftover food and drink. You feel like cleaning up, you don't want to be useless, last night seems to have been nice, you didn't talk much, it all went ahead without words. But: It's not easy to clean up when you're on strange turf. How to know the proper way to separate the garbage? You used to assess strange apartments by their books and their records. Wherever you went: A quick glance along the bookshelves. And you knew. But you can no longer rely on that. Everyone's books and music are increasingly alike. Waste separation is the thing now. Where do you put the paper, the glass, the organic waste? You look all around, you peer under the sink, but there are no options, just a single container. No other choices. Quietly, you put on your shoes.

OVERLOAD

The sea on the one side, cliffs on the other. Highway, high beams. The music helps me keep my eyes open. Short songs about love that hurts. *It's only midnight. Seduce me, honey, let's kill some time. She'll never know we've been together. It's only midnight, let's go wild. Do you think of me when you're with her? But before you take my clothes off, you should know that my body does come with a soul, and as I give you one, you get the other as well.*

All love affairs come to an unhappy end, is what the songs say. It's all so far away, also so close. In the distance, the flickering lights of a gas station. I bide my time. Looking. My breath fogs up the window. Therefore I am. I've been thinking about it for quite a while, now I know. He'll stop for gas. I'll take my purse and say I need to go to the ladies' room, I'll get in another car, I bet there's one open and ready, and I'll start on another journey. I'm sure there are other journeys. I'm sure he'll understand. So much music, explaining everything. All love affairs come to an unhappy end, is what the songs say.

HIGHWAY, HIGH BEAMS

"It's no good for a woman to travel alone," he said just before she got out. She didn't look back. "I know," she said, closing the door. "It's dangerous," he added, speaking to the closed door, then shrugged and started the car. Whoever picks her up here is bound to be dangerous, he thought. Dangerous because only dangerous people pick up hitchhikers in dangerous places like this.

I know, she thought again, I know that all right. It's no good for a woman to travel alone. It's dangerous. Luckily I still have that knife in my purse. I didn't want to leave it behind. I wiped it thoroughly, but you never know. They still could've found something when they found him. Dangerous, sure it is, all sorts of things can happen when you're hitchhiking. You never know who'll pick you up. And you never know what you'll be like when you get out again.

I WRITE THESE WORDS

in a hotel in the old part of a prosperous city. My room has a balcony, a TV set, an electric kettle, a phone, and a double bed, even though I'm alone. I've brought my laptop and cell phone with me. In hotels like this I always get the urge to write a letter or send some e-mails. As I boot up the computer to get online, a siren wails beneath my window. From my balcony I watch a prostrate young man being put on a stretcher. His girlfriend is crying hysterically. Giving it their best at first, the paramedics eventually let the boy slump back to the ground. The way they handle him is rougher now, they've given up, it's over. Overdose. The girl has gone quiet and taken a step backward, knowing her tears can no longer make a difference.

I write these words, which also can't make a difference. The double bed will go on being empty, and so will the room, except for me, of course. I'll go on wanting to send an e-mail, but I won't, because it will make me sad if there's no reply. The boy on the stretcher will go on being dead, and his girlfriend will go on knowing her tears couldn't change anything. I write these words, and now they can't change either. Nor can you, when you've finally read this, change them. They're here now. And the boy is gone. The paramedics have long since folded up the stretcher, washed their hands, gone home, they have their own lives, there's quite a few dead bodies in the streets. His girlfriend has gone home as well, her life has possibly changed, she may have joined a commune, gotten her act together, she may be someplace else now, perhaps looking after your children at the kindergarten. As you read this, somebody else is occupying that room, and maybe there's no siren wailing and nobody dying beneath that window. It's better that way. That way these words have a happier ending. Sometimes it's better if nothing happens.

WORDS MATTER

Reaching my room, I looked at the card the desk clerk had given me. There was a picture, there was a phone number, and there was something written in a language I didn't understand.

I dialed the number. A woman answered. We switched to English straight away. "I feel a bit lonely," I said. "Would you come up to my room?" The woman was silent for quite a while. "Are you sure you know who you're calling?" she finally asked. "Well, there's a picture on the card. I assumed it was you?" "It is, but—did you read what it says below? Words matter." "So you're not . . ." "No, I'm not."

I was at a loss. "What then? What can we do?" "I'll listen to your story," she said. My head was spinning. I think I read a short story or something with exactly this same premise, once. It didn't end well. "I don't have a story." "Sure you do, everybody has one. You wouldn't be staying in this hotel if you didn't." What did that mean? My reasons for being there were most definitely not—

"Won't you come up to my room anyway?" I tried again. I could hear her shake her head no. "You have my number. When you're ready, call me. I'll listen to you."

Listen? *Listen?* Disgusted, I put the receiver down as far from me as possible, on the edge of the bed. Why would anyone want to listen to what's happened to someone else, a total stranger? For money, of course. Disgusting. Money again. It can buy everything, everything except—

I sit in my room. The street below seethes with life. I should get up, I should go out, mingle with people, I keep telling myself. I don't get up. I fiddle with the card, wondering how to begin. What my first sentence should be. A good beginning is important. Words matter.

THE MOMENT OF DECISION

The man decides that things can't go on like this. The man realizes all the women he knows only want to be friends; even the ones who sleep over only sleep over because they've been rejected by his best friend. The man quits his job, leases his apartment. The man goes abroad. The man travels a long time and is silent, people speak to him, he answers as briefly as possible. The man is finally tired, the man stops somewhere, the man rents a room. The man watches the girl making his bed. The man feels something inside him stir, something he thought he had left far behind in the past. The man tells the girl she is beautiful. The man is glad when the girl laughs and thanks him. The man asks if she has time for a drink after work. The man is pleased when the girl says she does. The man thinks it perfectly all right when, after the drink, or rather, the drinks, the girl declines to come up to his room, or rather, the bed she has made. The man tells himself it's really too soon. The man is glad when he sees the girl in the hallway the next morning and she smiles. The man is in love. The man decides not to travel anymore; this place is just as good as the next one, or better, rather, far better. The man takes the girl out to dinner many times, out for drinks, out on trips on her days off. Then, when she has two days off, the man invites her on a longer trip. After dinner in a faraway town the man asks her if she feels like staying, like spending the night. The man is happy when she says she does. The man knows: It has to be in some other hotel, not the one she works in. The man pays for the room, leaves a tip, orders drinks up to the room. The man enjoys feeling the looks of envy on his back as he climbs the stairs to their room. The man doesn't understand why the girl starts crying when she sees the bed meant for two, them, and not one, him. The man thinks: This is love, a surprise, it always catches you by surprise, and it did her too. The man tells himself: You have to live for something larger than yourself. The man walks up to her, places his hands on her shoulders. The girl looks at him, she looks at him for a long time, then she crosses herself and starts undoing her blouse. The girl asks him: Will you always love me? The man thinks: Yes, that is the right question for this moment. The man is happy.

ON PAPER

He was one of those men who went out for a paper and never came back. For a long time he didn't know why. Now he did. It was to meet her, he told himself. And now he wanted to go back. But she wouldn't go with him. No. She put it differently. I want to but I can't, she'd said. He didn't understand. Where there's a will there's a way, he said. She didn't seem to understand. Even though he spoke slowly and used simple words. Even though he promised to pay for her ticket and buy her shoes and clothes like those in the pictures she'd torn out of magazines. She still wouldn't.

Then, one evening when a tropical downpour turned the streets into torrents of mud and they really couldn't go out for dinner, she told him she didn't exist. What do you mean you don't exist? he asked. Sure you exist, what have I been feeling next to me all these nights? Next to you yes, but not on paper, she said, I don't have a passport, I can't go anywhere.

You don't? We'll have one made up, he said, I'll arrange everything, we'll leave. She kept shaking her head. You can't arrange it, I don't have a birth certificate either, my mom and dad didn't have any papers filed for me, it wasn't done in our village, it didn't matter, who knew I'd end up in the city, it wasn't necessary in our village. Now they're gone, and our village where the people knew me is gone, it's too late now, I'm in the city now, you're the only one who knows me, but not by the name my people used to know me by, I've changed my name to avoid being recognized in case anyone else came here and started talking about me.

But, she said, looking into his startled eyes, it doesn't matter anyway. We are here, together, alive, what more could we wish for? Indeed, alive, and on my paper, he thought, fingering the wad of bills in his pocket, which once again would not purchase his ticket back home, to that newsstand where his newspapers were still waiting for him.

OTHER PATHS

He said: I can sleep in a chair. I can go to bed after the last guest has left and get up before the first one arrives. I can bring in customers for you. If white people see one of their own sitting here already, they'll be sure to come in. You can triple your prices. Sure, in that case the locals won't come anymore. You have to choose. Weigh your options. The difference in price times the quantity, as they say in the business. Or I can be near-invisible if you like, I can cook and wash up, you won't even know I'm there.

They said: What are you doing here? You don't belong here. Why don't you stay with your own people?

He said: My parents died. My wife left. There were no children.

Friends, they said.

I had a friend, he said, but, well, my wife left with my friend.

Why here? they said. Why our village? Not many people come here. Certainly none of your kind.

Exactly, he said. That's why.

Hmm, they said. There's room over there. Do you have a blanket? He shook his head.

They gave him a blanket. We'll take it out of your pay, they said.

He nodded. On payday, go ahead, he said.

You have no money? they said.

He smiled. Not anymore. My wife, my friend, the long journey here . . .

Do you want a bowl of rice? they said.

If you can spare it, he said.

They laughed. Spare, a bowl of rice! It really was about time a white man came to our village. Welcome, friend.

He flinched. Is there another village further on, even though the path ends here? he asked.

STAINS

He was dusty, badly scratched, his T-shirt was covered with discolored yellow stains. "I was thrown off the train." "Thrown off? Just like that?" "My backpack. They kept it." "What are you going to do now?" "Could I have something to drink first?"

We poured, he splashed water on his face, and the sand began to flake off. "More, please." We exchanged glances—there wasn't enough water left even for us, but that wasn't what concerned us. Next he'll want to ride with us, we thought. And our jeep was so crowded we could hardly stand one another as it was.

"Things like this happen," we tried to offer him whatever comfort our detached perspective might provide, "if one travels a lot." He shook his head. "This is my first time. My father used to travel a lot, but me—the first time."

We exchanged glances. Those stains. We travel a lot too, but we're careful to do it in style. "How come he didn't come this time? Too old, is he?" We're quite mature ourselves, we thought, seasoned veterans but not too old to hit the road, and if everything goes well we'll never be—

"He did come. In a way." In what way? Where is he? "In my backpack. In a tin." He's lost his mind, we thought, what's he talking about—

"He died. And left a will. Leaving me everything, so long as I scatter his ashes in the desert. And so—" His ashes? "In my backpack. All packed up. In a tea tin."

And so they've robbed you of everything. Well, you can always lie, you can always say that you were thrown off the train only after you'd . . . the only people who could give you away are the ones who threw you off the train, and us of course, but we . . . "Well," we said. "Well. Your father used to travel. He'd understand. And besides, what are those people going to do with a tin like that. When they open it, when they see there's no tea in it, they'll throw it away. And here . . ." We spread our arms. Sand, nothing but sand.

He nodded. "I've been through all that in my mind, I've been walking a while," he said. "But. How will I *know*?" We shrugged. How should we know how he would know? "If I do what you suggest, anything I get will be tainted, stained. It wouldn't be *fair*."

Hmm. What now? Come with us, we'll manage somehow, at least as far as the town, it'll be easier then—it's easier to think after you've taken a shower.

He shook his head.

"I can't go back until I've found my father. And made sure everything's okay."

Well, we thought, a needle in a haystack, that's doable, but dust in an ocean of sand, that's, well . . . "Is there anything else we can do for you?" we asked.

"If I could have a little more water, please," he murmured and began turning toward the horizon.

IN PASSING

That rock. That came crashing. Through the window. In passing. Came crashing. Through the window. Of the rushing train. With bars on its windows. Because of the ones out there. Who throw rocks. At trains rushing past. Because they're angry. Because they're outside. Not moving. That rock. Hurtling past the bars. Past the women seated by the window. Next to the bars. That rock. That someone had thrown. Hurtled past. Past everyone. Except me. Who was seated by the door. Virtually outside the compartment. Out of reach, as it were. That rock. Came crashing. With the anger of all the ones out there. Anger at all who go past. Came crashing. Past everyone. But me. Who had come from far away. That rock. Thrown from far away. Hitting me. Direct hit. Not going past. Breaking my nose. And the women screamed. That rock. Covered in mud. Which splattered around. And mixed with blood. My blood. That rock.

I now carry in my bag. Thinking, then: When I take this train again I'll throw it back. But years passed. I never traveled in that direction again. Now I watch the trains go past and think: Past. But I do have a rock in my bag.

DISCOURSE

The professor looks at her student, thinking: He wants me, I'm still beautiful. The student looks at his professor, thinking: She'd have me, I'm smart enough. The professor thinks about her years of attractiveness running out. The student thinks about the smart people accepting him sooner than he'd hoped. The professor tells herself she could lock the door, it's late on a hot afternoon, exams are over. The student tells himself everyone has gone home, exams are over, nobody would notice. The professor considers whether she should ask anything else. The student wonders whether what happens or doesn't happen will affect his grade. The professor does not want allowances made. The student does not want allowances made. The professor only wants to be sure that it happens because of her and not because of her position. The student only wants to be sure that his grade is what he *really* deserves.

LEARNING

I used to be a university professor, now I live on the street. Could you spare some change so I could have a square meal and do my laundry?

He had been practicing the two sentences in his mind for a long time. His lectures, though, continued. True, no students attended, and hadn't for a long time, but nobody appeared to notice, and the doorman still nodded to him every time he saw him struggling to insert his key in the lecture-room door. *I have to learn,* he thought, *someday, someday it'll come in handy. I have to learn.*

CROSSING THE HORIZON

It was only in the afternoon that he noticed he hadn't taken everything. His sunglasses weren't there. And he wouldn't be able to go to sleep without them. He drove back, thinking: Is she going to laugh if I ring the bell and tell her what I'm missing? Is she going to throw them at me from the fourth floor? He couldn't even hold it against her, not after everything that had happened. Is she just going to hand them over coolly, without a word, without *don't come here anymore*, without *I hope this is the last I see of you*, without *drop by sometime*, without *good to see you again*? Is he going to hear someone else moving around in her apartment? Suddenly, unexpectedly, anything was possible.

Her apartment block appeared on the horizon, and their, *her* bed linen on the balcony. Drying, absorbing the sunrays, a serene image of peace and quiet. As though their last few days together had never happened. As though he had never lain between those sheets. As though they were waiting fresh and ready for someone to come, for the right one to come.

He pulled up beneath the building and sat mustering the strength to get out of the car. Looking at what was spread out on the balcony. Looking for imprints of himself on the sheets. His eyes watered, he wasn't used to so much light. Slowly, little by little, it'll get easier, he told himself.

He kept looking, the hours going by. He would have rung the bell, except that he didn't want to know what was written on it now. Maybe, he thought, things will just work out, maybe she'll step out onto the balcony to take down the laundry, see my car below, come down, bring me my shades, tell me to come on up, say everything's different now, brand new—

She didn't come out, and when he again looked up to see if the laundry was still on the balcony, he realized it had gotten dark out, she wouldn't see him now even if she did come out onto the balcony. What now? What should he do? He knew he wouldn't be able to go to sleep without his sunglasses. He no longer had a bed, but he still had his car. If he kept driving in the right direction, nonstop, he thought, the sun would never set. Speed, speed was of the essence, he just had to reach the right speed. He turned on the ignition.

CRACKS

Many stories have happened. This is one of them. You have a wife, you have some kids, you have a job, you have a car, you have a house in the suburbs. It looks like you'll die happy, your children will cry at your funeral, and your neighbors will be sorry you're gone. Then one night as you're driving home in the last evaporating tendrils of light, going no faster than usual, there's a thump, you hit something. You haven't seen anything, there was just this thud against your car. You stop, you get out to see what's happened. There's a child lying under your car, seven, eight years old, you've got one just like him waiting for you at home, he could've been yours. He doesn't move. A pool of blood is forming under his head.

You cry out, bend down, feel for his pulse, find nothing. You look around, there's no one there, the street is deserted. You drive along this street every day without knowing anyone—a housing development, gray and disheveled. There's no one watching, all the lights are out.

What now? What do you do when something like this happens to you? You know: If the child were to moan a little, it would all be simple. You'd load him in your car and rush him to the hospital. Or call for an ambulance. But you can see there's nothing to save. When you calm down a little you see the streetlights haven't even come on yet. You see there are no cars in the street. You turn and look around to see if anyone's coming, if anyone's lurking behind the dumpsters, watching. But there's no one anywhere.

You'd like to call someone, but whom? Besides, your phone battery has suddenly run out and you realize that nobody would answer even if it did still work. You look at the child again. He seems to have been lying there for hours, his face has grown colorless, the blood under his head has dried. You look around again and the buildings along the street seem to be crumbling, the asphalt crackling, huge fissures appearing in the night sky, through which the void will begin to seep in at any moment. You're still holding your car keys, you look at them, you look at your car, and you know it will never move again. You drop the keys, they fall slowly into the dark beneath you and you're not even surprised when you don't hear the metal strike the asphalt. There's no sound left anywhere. No dogs barking, no televisions buzzing, no phones ringing. Again you bend over the child. He's getting tinier and tinier and more and more dried out, you look at your hands and wait for the cracks to appear on them too. You think: I had a wife, I had kids, it seemed I would die happy. Now things will happen differently. Many stories don't have happy endings. This is one of them.

THE MAN WHO DIDN'T THROW HIMSELF UNDER A TRAIN SPEAKS

I didn't want to fall in love. But I did. It didn't work out. I remember everything. How I threw the rings I'd bought us in the river and she got scared I'd hurt her if she refused me. Each and every note I stuck under her windshield wipers. I wrote so much, on every one of them, even though the pieces of paper were so small. I gave all of myself. Burned my bridges. My wife said I was crazy, the kids were still small, I used to have a good job, what was I thinking, roaming the city all day long. I know what I had in mind. Running into her. But I never did. And even when I did, I pretended not to see her. Because I didn't know what to say. Because she'd told me: No more. So I didn't. I didn't want to. But then, after she'd thrown herself under the train, I heard. They said I had goaded her into it. That she cried every time the phone rang. Because she always thought it was me.

But it wasn't. Not always. They said that it was my fault. But I didn't want that. I only wanted her to hear me out. So I could tell her about us. Once and for all. One more time. But she wouldn't have any of it. She left and never said she was leaving. If she had, it would've been different. I would've told her. But I didn't. Because she didn't say. So now I go to the station, every day, to see if maybe I can leave town. My wife won't let me near the kids anymore. She has it in writing, too. Says I'm dangerous. Likely to do something. But I'm not going to do anything. It wouldn't change a thing. Maybe she never really died. I didn't go to the funeral; they said I'd better not. Maybe there never was a funeral. Maybe she's waiting at some station, waiting for me to arrive. I just don't know which train to take. I look at them and can't make up my mind. I just look.

A DAY I LOVED YOU

I lay there with my eyes closed, waiting for my husband
to vacate his half of the bed. To go to work, of course.
He'll get a sandwich on the corner. He'll have a coffee
during his first meeting. Then he'll call home. To make
sure that I'm still here, and haven't run away. I'm not
going to. I'm going to open that box of old snapshots
again. There were no hard drives back in those days.
I'll go through it all photo by photo, and with each one
think: That was a day I loved you.

ALL OVER

At first he spent his nights online, "socializing" more and more, without any of his exchanges ever becoming profound: Everyone was just seeking a little comfort, a few lines' or one night's worth; nobody would discuss the big questions with him. When at last he thought he'd found a kindred spirit, when he worked up his courage and arranged a meeting in a coffee shop, the disappointment was mutual. The guy who showed up clutching the agreed-upon Lorca had obviously been expecting someone else, probably a teenage girl hiding behind the digital persona of a grown-up man.

He no longer logged on after that. Women whose husbands had walked out on them for younger women; men whose wives had left, taking everything, including the children—the flames of the war between the sexes flickered on the monitor. It was one big run-on litany of advice given just so people could unload their own stories of woe. He wanted no part of it. He'd had enough.

Now his nights were longer. Going home in the evening was getting harder day by day. For a while he continued to avoid the mess in the kitchen, then decided it was time to clean it up. He swept up the spilled flour and pasta, mopped up the puddles of oil and wine, picked up the pieces of broken glass. The stains on the walls could not be wiped off. He tried whitewashing them, but they always bled through. The tip he found on the Web was to use a scraper. So now whenever he got the urge to think about what the hell had gone wrong, he'd go to the wall and start scraping. At night the stains seemed to shrink; in the morning he'd paint them over, inspect them in the evening, and at night scrape away at them again. If at all, things progressed at such a slow pace that he never noticed whether he was accomplishing anything. He looked at the stains on the wall, thinking: Maybe I should start all over again. As a house painter. Then I'd know where I'd gone wrong. With my painting, of course.

THIRTY YEARS

It's awful how time changes things, she thought. Everything used to be open, it seemed like everything was still ahead of us, but then it's all over and it all comes down to a moment when there are no longer two paths in front of you.

It's awful how a man you've loved for so many years changes, she thought. His skin used to be smooth as glass and warm as cotton. Now it's furrowed like the earth and cold as ice.

It's awful how a woman who's loved someone for so many years changes, she thought. Her hand used to caress, now it holds a knife.

SPINNING

His time at the turntables started off well. He'd found the right vibe, the energy mounted, the girls began undoing buttons and rolling up their tank tops, the crowd at the bar thickened, the bartenders gave him the thumbs up. Then he messed up a mix and at the drop of a hat everything changed. After moving listlessly through a few more steps, the crowd retreated to the dim corners off the edges of the floor. He changed the beat, pretending he'd made the break on purpose. Nobody bought it. A blonde dressed in dental floss, essentially, came up to hiss something at him. He spread his arms in a gesture that was meant to say *it's my call, deal with it.* With a dismissive flourish she grabbed her glittery coat off a seat. She motioned and a bunch of similar looking girls joined her on her way out.

He browsed among the records, thinking of a way to proceed. You make one wrong move, miss the groove once, and you're out. The end of the road. But there may be others. He'll have to get out of the game, go back to university, tell his professor that he's ready now to hand in his doctoral thesis. Some things come to an end a bit sooner than one anticipates, so it's important to notice when they're over. He selected a familiar slow track. The guy behind the bar gave him a nod and started stacking up glasses.

A SINGLE NIGHT

You go to bed a bank mogul, you wake up a rickshaw driver. You wonder: How is that possible? Where did my villa disappear to? A single night and everything's changed. Now you sleep in the street, putting your one pair of shoes under your head so they won't be stolen. Nobody believes you when you tell them you used to be rich only a little while ago. They laugh, making you wonder how you learned their language overnight and what happened to your own native tongue. You can't remember it anymore, which precludes going to any embassy for help. Also, your skin has turned strangely dark, and you understand why nobody believes that you used to be a man whose decisions affected the lives of so many people, while now you spend your time waiting around for someone who'll let you pull them down the street for a bowl of rice.

The nights are tough. Every night you hope you'll wake up back in your own bed again, wake up to the realization this is all just a bad dream. But you don't. And then, one day, as you wait around as usual, a ring glints in the mud at your feet. You pick it up, wipe it off, watch it glitter. It could be gold. You quickly hide it in your shoe. You know that caution is needed. If anyone finds out you have it, you might never wake up again.

All your sorrow is gone. You know: From now on things will only get better. A single night and everything's changed. You think: If this ring is the real thing, if this is the start of a new fortune, I'll never sleep again. It's too dangerous. A single night and everything's changed.

I CAN'T DECIDE,

me, who used to make so many decisions, he said to himself. And then he was angry when the vending machine ate his money. He shook it, but the soda can still wouldn't come tumbling down. Finally he gave up and drank some tap water. No brand, but it quenched his thirst. He took all the coins from the tip plate outside the bathroom door, to get even for losing out to the machine. The thought crossed his mind that he should charge for lost time, though if they paid his standard fee in small change, he wouldn't be able to carry so many coins.

A free daily was stuck behind his windshield wiper. *Fund Crash. Investors Frantic. Tycoon on the Run.* No comment, he thought. That was someone else. Not him. He had a different name now, different papers, a different appearance. And accounts in different places all over the world. Among which he was now unable to decide. Because he had never been anyplace, really. Always in his office, at his accounts. He'll have to choose sometime, though. But not yet. He can go on driving, the airport is still far away. Sometime.

EXPERTS

They flagged us down at the first exit off the highway. When they first started waving I was going to drive by, but then I saw they had guns. Pointed at us.

"Where are you going? Don't you know there's a war on?" they yelled. "What war?" I asked. "Between us and them," they said, nodding knowingly at one another. "I didn't know," I admitted contritely. "I haven't heard."

They nodded. "Sure, there are no reports about us. We're not newsworthy. And it suits *them* better if everything seems to be all right. Because otherwise there'd be more of *us*."

"If we shoot you," someone said, "we'll get media coverage. We'll send your body parts to all the news agencies. There's no way they can ignore that." The others nodded knowingly.

I shook my head. "Bad publicity," I said. "Believe me, I work in the field. Public relations. We're on our way to a conference. Chopping off limbs, that's so . . . prehistoric. They'll think you're all a bunch of brainless barbarians. You don't want that, do you?"

They exchanged glances and shook their heads. "I didn't think so," I said. "You have to do this differently, take a different approach. Times are different."

"What do you suggest?" they asked despondently.

Hmm. What do we suggest?

"We're in public relations, all of us. We're on our way to a conference. We're organizing a workshop there to see who can come up with the best promo idea, and we were just complaining that we didn't have a good product to pitch. And voilà: Here we have a war that can't get media coverage. We'll come back and tell you what we come up with. That way you're happy, we're happy. A win-win solution, as we say in the business."

They were happy. We'd won. "Deal?" "Deal."

They cheered enthusiastically as we pulled away. They could've fired a few rounds in the air, I thought, that would've made our good-byes even more festive. Maybe their guns weren't real after all. Maybe they'd taken us for a ride. Another pro bono job! But we weren't sure.

That's why we didn't go back to ask. And—we'll have to do that damn workshop too. Maybe the whole thing *is* for real. Maybe there really is a war going on that we know nothing about.

SUNDAY DINNERS

A long time ago, before the war, generals, good friends of my grandfather's, used to attend my grandmother's dinners, she remembers. Those days are over; a lot of time has passed. The generals of today couldn't care less about congenial Sunday dinners; they sit in their offices, clicking on screens, they don't seem to care about my grandmother and her famous stuffed duck. Understandably, these days, my grandmother can't just sit around waiting for the next war. Frantically, she hoards the ingredients for stuffed duck in her cellar—her deep freezer is full of headless bodies in plastic wrap, and she's bought an oil generator because it's common knowledge that electricity is one of the first things to go in wartime; the oil should last for a few Sunday dinners at least. On Sundays, my grandmother calls up her grandchildren, one by one: "Will you come when the war starts?" she asks. "Will you come?" We explain that there could be complications, there could be road-blocks, there could be shooting, someone might even be drafted. "I'm not eating my duck by myself," grandmother sobs into the receiver, "not all by myself, dinners like that make no sense. I hate war, I hate wars like this, wars used to be *comme il faut* in the old days, they didn't interfere with my stuffed duck." Those days are over, Grandma, we explain patiently, it's all mixed up now, no one knows what it will be like when it happens. Grandmother's whimpers slowly subside, we put down our receivers and go over to our closets, concerned, wanting to make sure that everything is in place, the weapons all loaded and the safeties all off, ready, we must be ready now, nobody knows when it will happen, when it happens.

I THINK

I think the war is over. I think we'll be starting over. I don't think I've hurt anyone. I think I can leave this place. I think I'm still a child. I think my hands are no longer covered in blood. I think I've survived.

THE POWER OF WORDS

They say: You can't blame the tiger for eating the antelope. Eating antelopes is its nature. It's nice, being a tiger: the endless grasslands, plenty of antelopes waiting for you to get hungry. Night is coming; you'll fall asleep, sleep, and dream of being a tiger. Now test your power in a different way: Explain to another tiger that an antelope is a living, sentient being. Tell him: Picture this, you're not a tiger anymore, you're an antelope now, running from a tiger, your strength is failing but you run, you run, the tiger is gaining on you, you think you should've run in the other direction but it's too late now, the tiger is coming from that direction. And when your legs buckle and the tiger finally catches up, as is bound to happen, you, the antelope, say to the tiger: "You're not going to eat me, are you? Meat is murder. Your steak had feelings once, you know." And the tiger stops. Thinks.

HOME FROM XPAND

"I'm sick and tired of being holed up behind the screen all the time, huffing and puffing, roaring into the theater and shaking the seats, without ever seeing the movie," hissed the 3D monster just before ripping off the head of the first patron.

VIDEOTAPES

All those movies that played. All those movies. I knew they weren't true. That truth lay elsewhere. But. All those movies. So many colors. Dazzling me though I kept closing my eyes. Things go on moving beyond closed eyelids. The world is orderly beyond closed eyelids. But when I open them, things change. That's when I scream and rant and rave and never *ever* get an answer to the only question that matters: Where, *where* did I put my videotapes?

THE STONES MEET MY GRANDMA

Nobody knew who the woman was when she leaped onto the stage. Who is she, what is she doing there? The security guards have gotten distracted again, busy watching all the bare skin in the front rows. Will she just try to kiss Mick like all of them do, or will she go for the mike and shout something? Look at her. The way she eludes capture. What's going to happen now? Is she going to yell *Mick* (or possibly *Keith*, but definitely not *Charlie*), *I love you*, and try to fling herself into his arms, or is she going to say something terrible to the crowd, something so terrible that the Prime Minister will have to make an appearance on television to address the issue?

The close-up: you can see the microphone sway, Mick's spittle dripping from it. The woman evades the hands reaching for her and, cupping her own around her mouth, leans close to Mick's ear. For a moment the band seems to have frozen: Charlie's sticks hover in the air before resuming their descent, while Mick grins with satisfaction. I'm not making this up. I have it all on tape, it's part of a documentary, fifty-eight minutes and sixteen seconds in, at home we've watched it umpteen times.

Yes, we've watched it umpteen times, asking: What did you say to him, Grandma? *What did you say to him?* And Grandma always just smiled, kept on smiling even after she lost all her teeth and saliva would dribble down her chin whenever she curved her lips, making us look away. Now she no longer talks; when we come to visit she just motions and we know: She'd like to watch that scene again. We'll never know what she said to Mick; maybe she actually just said *I love you*, maybe she said something else, documentaries don't show everything, God knows what happened after the cameras stopped rolling, maybe Mick is our grandfather, because our mother never did learn who her father was, maybe this is the key, maybe Mick's other children should give a portion of all their villas and yachts to us. Maybe, if you're in the right place at the right time, too many things are possible.

COMING

Don't be afraid, Mom. I won't take up too much of your time. Sure, it'll hurt. But that will pass. And you'll be glad when it's over. You won't forget. You might if it didn't hurt. Pain has a way of becoming engraved in one's memory. It hurts me too, in case you didn't know. I'm scared too. But I don't understand what you're thinking. You press your hands on the walls of my world, palpating them to feel me move, afraid when I lie too still, sleeping, scared that I'm gone.

I'm here. I feel. I dream. I breathe. I'll come. Things will be different when I come. They won't matter anymore. Your old, cramped room. You think you can't go back there. But it won't matter once I come. I'll be tiny enough for you to take there. You'll be smaller too. The whole world will have shrunk. For a while we'll be enough, just the two of us. You won't think of him anymore. Why he never showed up. Why he never comes around anymore. Why he never calls. Why he never leaves flowers on your doorstep. Wildflowers. The smell of crushed grass. The juices on your clothes. That's all gone. A lot of things are gone. I'm not. I've stayed. I'll stay on. I'll come out of you. I came out of him too, but that doesn't matter anymore. He'll be excised, in a way. From you. And I'll have come. And stayed. It'll work. From now on. And you'll tell everyone when they ask, "Whose is he?" "Mine," you'll say.

That's the way it's going to be at first. Then it'll change again. I'll be leaving. Becoming my own person. And you'll be hurt again. But don't worry. Everything changes. The pain goes away. Its edges wear off. And things work out. Don't listen to the whispers behind your back: "She's on her own." You're not on your own. I'm here.

Don't worry. It'll work out. Somehow. I'm here. I feel. I dream. I breathe. I'm coming.

BECOMING

When I become a father, thinks the boy, I'll make sure I stay a boy. Because a child needs a father who knows how to be a child.

When I become a father, thinks the boy, it will be different. That is: I'll be a different father. Because I will be the father of a child who will want a father who knows how to be a child.

When I become a father, thinks the boy, my child will be a different child. Because my child will have a father who knows how to be a child.

When I become a father, thinks the boy, I'll become a different child too. And my child will have a father who knows how to be a child. Who knows, thinks the boy, how to be a different child.

When I become a father, thinks the boy, my father just might become a different father, he might become a father who knows how to become a child.

When I become a father, thinks the child, tears drying on his face, the skin no longer stinging, everything becoming different, when I become a father, thinks the child.

A DARK AND STORMY NIGHT

But it wasn't a dark and stormy night at all. On the contrary: It was painfully bright. The liquid crystal sky was repeatedly torn by neon lightning, its glare blinding me. But I knew I couldn't stop, I knew I had to hurry on if I wanted to accomplish the task, and that there was no one, absolutely no one else who could do it for me: It was all up to me.

I jumped over another few fire pits and finally I saw her. Trembling, she waited to see who would reach her first: The monster or her rescuer. Her face brightened when she saw me. "It's you, Superboy, my savior, isn't it?" I nodded. "My strength has failed, I can no longer run." I slung her over my shoulder. "Don't worry," I said.

Dodging bullets, we sped from one level to the next.

"We won't make it," she moaned, "I'm very weak, and even your great strength isn't limitless."

"Don't worry. There," I pointed into the distance, "there's the door to safety."

But as I reached out for the door handle, there was a flash and I was plunged into darkness. My mother had unplugged the cable again!

"I was so close, Mom!" I groaned.

My mother shook her head. "Four hours is quite enough, Superboy. If you can't manage to save your damsel after all that time, you'd better just go out and play with your friends."

But Mom, I thought, you don't know anything. Out there, it's a dark and stormy night.

OFFICERS' DAUGHTERS

You would laugh at us when we practiced fretting chords on our guitars. Your fathers would give a shrill whistle from their balconies and you would hurry home for dinner. Then one evening our fingers managed to string together a melody and you began to hang around a little longer from then on. Your fathers glowered at what was going on below. They used to play the guitar themselves; they knew what was coming. You began to let yourselves be kissed on the mouth. Occasionally one of you would lift up her top. Your fathers would stroke their loaded weapons and suffer. They knew there was no turning back the tide, no matter how badly they wanted to. And you would come deeper and deeper into the woods. Occasionally you would talk about your fathers, saying things one wouldn't want to hear from his daughter.

We no longer brought our guitars with us; other things mattered now. One after another your fathers left, though some of them were still around long enough to pat your bulging bellies and murmur their good wishes. Sooner or later, the boys you gave birth to found those guitars stashed away in hidden corners. When they first strummed them, the strings gave off terrible sounds. But then they learned about tightening and loosening. New songs began.

In the evenings you wished your daughters would stay at home, but they were outside, laughing; you would get up, go over to the window and motion to us: Look what they're doing. We looked, we listened, not all the melodies unfamiliar. And thought: Whistle, I should whistle.

CUP OF COFFEE

You were at home. Safe. Under the covers. Dreaming of sleeping peacefully on a faraway shore. Simply enjoying it. Not understanding the clouds pressing down, hating the thunder. It was good when it was over. Good to be safe, at your place. Sweet coffee washes away the morning haze. Good coffee, from far away. Children haul sacks of the beans through the jungle. In twenty-three hours earning the price of an espresso at your corner café. Their homes are nailed together from rolled metal used for transporting waste products overseas. If they ever reach the shore, they wave at ships in the distance.

You've bitten yourself when you wanted to scream in your dream. The bitter taste needs to be washed away. You lift up the thick sweet liquid, its pulsing flow coming to rest inside of you. Life-bringing, it will give you the strength to get through whatever the day presses down upon you. It makes your mouth sticky. You won't shout. You won't talk. You'll wipe your mouth on the back of your hand, kiss the woman you live with, go out. Reality calls.

You'll hurry past your neighbors'. Hear activity behind their open door. There's more and more TV noise in the air. Increasing numbers of children spending hours and days on end in front of the set. Watching the glorious world of home shopping. As Allah bears no gifts, as Buddha is not a giver, they ask Santa for slimming belts. Their mothers caress their potbellies.

The air in the street, sticky and burning, makes you feel like you've plunged into the soda pop advertised in neon. Above all the familiar billboards, a new one. Large. The largest. *Global Player. Global Prayer. Global Payer.* You take notice, nod, agreeing with but not understanding the message.

The street is thick, congested, yet swift as a torrent. You watch the people. They eat silently and with concentration. Every bite counts. The soothing mechanical rhythm of mastication. Counterbalancing the weight of the world. The persistence of a machine. Forward.

Faster. Stronger. Some stand. Some fall. Everything intertwined. Everything structured. An influx of strength. You flow into liquid; if your form is fluid enough you can bypass any obstacle.

The day rises. You raise your hand without reaching anywhere, your gesture saying nothing, attracting no one's attention, only affirming the ongoing state of affairs. Something inside you separates, breaks off, starts on its journey, something of which you remain unaware. It wants to move forward, it wants out, rising, ascending along narrow, congested pathways, wanting you to take notice, to feel. Somewhere, somewhere up front, somewhere high up there's a strait that will not allow passage, there's an ambush waiting to constrict and stop the flow. For good, forever.

When you feel it, you start gasping for air, clutching at your body, finding no handhold, it slips out of your hands, too slick, the world quakes and implodes, you feel the fierceness of the final thud. The cup of coffee, you manage to think. I shouldn't have—a cup of coffee. One too many. No more. What now? Where to now? You, you up there, what's going on, do something. Not now, I don't want now, do something. One more time, differently. What use to the world is a man who hasn't seen the world? What's going on? Go on? Gone?

FINAL STATEMENT

As they gathered at the ruins of the company, he lied that he had a doctor's appointment. His coworkers were outraged. "Who do you think you are?" somebody hissed at his back. "You think you're any better than us?" "Together through thick and thin," somebody else muttered under his breath. He shuddered. It sounded like something a marriage counselor might say.

Somebody extracted the glass plate with the firm's logo. "Something to remember it by?" he asked. The other man shook his head. "Nothing should be remembered," flinging it through the window. It crashed majestically among some passersby, making a few of them look up and others hasten their step with a shrug—a sign of the times, lots of things getting thrown out of windows lately.

It brought the boss running from his office, where he'd been holed up these last few weeks. "Stop that," he began uncertainly. "Look, we've really done everything in our power—" Yeah, right, everything, he thought, but we broke off the hunger strike due to the lack of public interest, and canceled the self-immolations because of poor ratings. Of course, everyone in the firm had been relieved—what if they'd been taken seriously and actually had to douse themselves with gasoline? Things weren't so bad, in the end, not really—they all had nest eggs, or had already been moonlighting, or had a vegetable patch on the outskirts of town. They'd survive, what else could they do.

The boss waited to see how his words would go down. Nobody paid him any attention. They were opening bottles, all of them drinking, no reason not to now. The boss slipped back into his office as usual, his lock clicking into place.

I have to get to the doctor's, he thought. "I'm out of here. I'll see you around, I guess," he said. Nobody paid any attention to him either. "Maybe I'll drop in later," he said into the growing clatter. "If you guys are still here."

He went outside and looked at the glass shards on the ground in surprise. Something had shattered. How

come nobody sweeps up? he thought, annoyed. Somebody should. But I'm not getting into that now, I have
to go to the doctor's, I guess.

ON THE HOUSE OF HONOR

The café in the courtyard of his building reopened. The former owner had been found in the river, his feet encased in concrete. Debt, it was rumored. A matter of honor. He had avoided the place ever since, not wanting to look at the metal grill over the door. Until one day when he did look and the grill was gone. The door was open, and there was a man inside, dusting off chairs. That's a lot of dust, he thought. The man inside said: "Hi there. Come on in."

He had a coffee. It wasn't good. It tasted like mud, stale. He watched the man behind the bar open the cupboards one by one, as though checking out what was in each one, and racked his brains over where he'd seen him before.

He got up to pay for the coffee but the man inside said: "No. It's on me today. Everything is on me today. I've paid everything off."

As the man reached to clear away the coffee cup, a muddy rivulet trickled down from under his sleeve. Frowning, he wiped it off.

OWN STORIES

All these concentration-camp guards, reading books about the meaning of life. About enriching their inner world, about the gift of endless serenity. All these guards, tears coursing down their cheeks at such wonderful realizations while they wait to be relieved. All these guards, hoping that someday—years from now—life will give them an opportunity to write their own stories as well.

END OF THE NOVEL

—and then, alert, on guard, I stopped outside the Door. Only as the handle began to yield under the weight of my hand did I realize my journey was over, that only two things could be waiting behind this door: Nothing at all, or it—or, rather, *It*.

MARKS

All my lovers give me bookmarks. They seem to think I must read a lot. I put all the marks into the same book, the one I never open. When I can't sleep at night I think about how I should, how I *ought to* open it and see what I've marked. What would a story made up of only my marked pages be like? I never do it, though. Perhaps I don't—or so I think when the night feels just a little too long—because whatever this story might be like, it would be about its being all over already, and about the impossibility of adding any new marks. About there not having been any sense in reading this story in the first place. Because it's all happened before. That's why I just look at the tops of the bookmarks peeking out of the book. Thinking.

In 2010, the Slovenian Book Agency took a bold step toward solving the problem of how few literary works are now translated into English, initiating a program to provide financial support for a series dedicated to Slovenian literature at Dalkey Archive Press. Partially evolving from a relationship that Dalkey Archive and the Vilenica International Literary Festival had developed a few years previously, this new program begins with the publication of three Slovenian novels in its first year, and will go on to ensure that both classic and contemporary works from Slovenian are brought into English, while allowing the Press to undertake marketing efforts far exceeding what publishers can normally provide for works in translation.

Slovenia has always held a great reverence for literature, with the Slovenian national identity being forged through its fiction and poetry long before the foundation of the contemporary Republic: "It is precisely literature that has in some profound, subtle sense safeguarded the Slovenian community from the imperialistic appetites of stronger and more expansive nations in the region," writes critic Andrej Inkret. Never insular, Slovenian writing has long been in dialogue with the great movements of world literature, from the romantic to the experimental, seeing the literary not as distinct from the world, but as an integral means of perceiving and even amending it.

ANDREJ BLATNIK was born in Ljubljana in 1963. In addition to writing fiction and criticism, he is president of the jury of the Vilenica International Literary Prize, and has translated the work of Paul Bowles and others. His collection *Skinswaps* was translated into English in 1998.

TAMARA M. SOBAN was born in Ljubljana in 1962. Among other works, she is the translator of Andrej Blatnik's *Skinswaps*. Since 2002 she has worked as a translator and editor for the Museum of Modern Art in Ljubljana.

PETROS ABATZOGLOU, *What Does Mrs. Freeman Want?*
MICHAL AJVAZ, *The Golden Age.*
The Other City.
PIERRE ALBERT-BIROT, *Grabinoulor.*
YUZ ALESHKOVSKY, *Kangaroo.*
FELIPE ALFAU, *Chromos.*
Locos.
IVAN ÂNGELO, *The Celebration.*
The Tower of Glass.
DAVID ANTIN, *Talking.*
ANTÓNIO LOBO ANTUNES, *Knowledge of Hell.*
ALAIN ARIAS-MISSON, *Theatre of Incest.*
IFTIKHAR ARIF AND WAQAS KHWAJA, EDS., *Modern Poetry of Pakistan.*
JOHN ASHBERY AND JAMES SCHUYLER, *A Nest of Ninnies.*
HEIMRAD BÄCKER, *transcript.*
DJUNA BARNES, *Ladies Almanack.*
Ryder.
JOHN BARTH, *LETTERS.*
Sabbatical.
DONALD BARTHELME, *The King.*
Paradise.
SVETISLAV BASARA, *Chinese Letter.*
RENÉ BELLETTO, *Dying.*
MARK BINELLI, *Sacco and Vanzetti Must Die!*
ANDREI BITOV, *Pushkin House.*
ANDREJ BLATNIK, *You Do Understand.*
LOUIS PAUL BOON, *Chapel Road.*
My Little War.
Summer in Termuren.
ROGER BOYLAN, *Killoyle.*
IGNÁCIO DE LOYOLA BRANDÃO, *Anonymous Celebrity.*
The Good-Bye Angel.
Teeth under the Sun.
Zero.
BONNIE BREMSER, *Troia: Mexican Memoirs.*
CHRISTINE BROOKE-ROSE, *Amalgamemnon.*
BRIGID BROPHY, *In Transit.*
MEREDITH BROSNAN, *Mr. Dynamite.*
GERALD L. BRUNS, *Modern Poetry and the Idea of Language.*
EVGENY BUNIMOVICH AND J. KATES, EDS., *Contemporary Russian Poetry: An Anthology.*
GABRIELLE BURTON, *Heartbreak Hotel.*
MICHEL BUTOR, *Degrees.*
Mobile.
Portrait of the Artist as a Young Ape.
G. CABRERA INFANTE, *Infante's Inferno.*
Three Trapped Tigers.
JULIETA CAMPOS, *The Fear of Losing Eurydice.*
ANNE CARSON, *Eros the Bittersweet.*
ORLY CASTEL-BLOOM, *Dolly City.*
CAMILO JOSÉ CELA, *Christ versus Arizona.*
The Family of Pascual Duarte.
The Hive.
LOUIS-FERDINAND CÉLINE, *Castle to Castle.*
Conversations with Professor Y.
London Bridge.

Normance.
North.
Rigadoon.
HUGO CHARTERIS, *The Tide Is Right.*
JEROME CHARYN, *The Tar Baby.*
MARC CHOLODENKO, *Mordechai Schamz.*
JOSHUA COHEN, *Witz.*
EMILY HOLMES COLEMAN, *The Shutter of Snow.*
ROBERT COOVER, *A Night at the Movies.*
STANLEY CRAWFORD, *Log of the S.S. The Mrs Unguentine.*
Some Instructions to My Wife.
ROBERT CREELEY, *Collected Prose.*
RENÉ CREVEL, *Putting My Foot in It.*
RALPH CUSACK, *Cadenza.*
SUSAN DAITCH, *L.C.*
Storytown.
NICHOLAS DELBANCO, *The Count of Concord.*
NIGEL DENNIS, *Cards of Identity.*
PETER DIMOCK, *A Short Rhetoric for Leaving the Family.*
ARIEL DORFMAN, *Konfidenz.*
COLEMAN DOWELL, *The Houses of Children.*
Island People.
Too Much Flesh and Jabez.
ARKADII DRAGOMOSHCHENKO, *Dust.*
RIKKI DUCORNET, *The Complete Butcher's Tales.*
The Fountains of Neptune.
The Jade Cabinet.
The One Marvelous Thing.
Phosphor in Dreamland.
The Stain.
The Word "Desire."
WILLIAM EASTLAKE, *The Bamboo Bed.*
Castle Keep.
Lyric of the Circle Heart.
JEAN ECHENOZ, *Chopin's Move.*
STANLEY ELKIN, *A Bad Man.*
Boswell: A Modern Comedy.
Criers and Kibitzers, Kibitzers and Criers.
The Dick Gibson Show.
The Franchiser.
George Mills.
The Living End.
The MacGuffin.
The Magic Kingdom.
Mrs. Ted Bliss.
The Rabbi of Lud.
Van Gogh's Room at Arles.
ANNIE ERNAUX, *Cleaned Out.*
LAUREN FAIRBANKS, *Muzzle Thyself.*
Sister Carrie.
LESLIE A. FIEDLER, *Love and Death in the American Novel.*
JUAN FILLOY, *Op Oloop.*
GUSTAVE FLAUBERT, *Bouvard and Pécuchet.*
KASS FLEISHER, *Talking out of School.*
FORD MADOX FORD, *The March of Literature.*
JON FOSSE, *Aliss at the Fire.*
Melancholy.

CHRISTINE SCHUTT, *Nightwork*.
GAIL SCOTT, *My Paris*.
DAMION SEARLS, *What We Were Doing and Where We Were Going*.
JUNE AKERS SEESE,
Is This What Other Women Feel Too?
What Waiting Really Means.
BERNARD SHARE, *Inish*.
Transit.
AURELIE SHEEHAN,
Jack Kerouac Is Pregnant.
VIKTOR SHKLOVSKY, *Knight's Move*.
A Sentimental Journey: Memoirs 1917–1922.
Energy of Delusion: A Book on Plot.
Literature and Cinematography.
Theory of Prose.
Third Factory.
Zoo, or Letters Not about Love.
CLAUDE SIMON, *The Invitation*.
PIERRE SINIAC, *The Collaborators*.
JOSEF ŠKVORECKÝ, *The Engineer of Human Souls*.
GILBERT SORRENTINO,
Aberration of Starlight.
Blue Pastoral.
Crystal Vision.
Imaginative Qualities of Actual Things.
Mulligan Stew.
Pack of Lies.
Red the Fiend.
The Sky Changes.
Something Said.
Splendide-Hôtel.
Steelwork.
Under the Shadow.
W. M. SPACKMAN,
The Complete Fiction.
ANDRZEJ STASIUK, *Fado*.
GERTRUDE STEIN,
Lucy Church Amiably.
The Making of Americans.
A Novel of Thank You.
LARS SVENDSEN, *A Philosophy of Evil*.
PIOTR SZEWC, *Annihilation*.
GONÇALO M. TAVARES, *Jerusalem*.
LUCIAN DAN TEODOROVICI,
Our Circus Presents . . .
STEFAN THEMERSON, *Hobson's Island*.
The Mystery of the Sardine.
Tom Harris.
JOHN TOOMEY, *Sleepwalker*.
JEAN-PHILIPPE TOUSSAINT,
The Bathroom.
Camera.
Monsieur.
Running Away.
Self-Portrait Abroad.
Television.
DUMITRU TSEPENEAG,
Hotel Europa.
The Necessary Marriage.
Pigeon Post.
Vain Art of the Fugue.
ESTHER TUSQUETS, *Stranded*.

DUBRAVKA UGRESIC,
Lend Me Your Character.
Thank You for Not Reading.
MATI UNT, *Brecht at Night*.
Diary of a Blood Donor.
Things in the Night.
ÁLVARO URIBE AND OLIVIA SEARS, EDS.,
Best of Contemporary Mexican Fiction.
ELOY URROZ, *Friction*.
The Obstacles.
LUISA VALENZUELA, *He Who Searches*.
MARJA-LIISA VARTIO,
The Parson's Widow.
PAUL VERHAEGHEN, *Omega Minor*.
BORIS VIAN, *Heartsnatcher*.
LLORENÇ VILLALONGA, *The Dolls' Room*.
ORNELA VORPSI, *The Country Where No One Ever Dies*.
AUSTRYN WAINHOUSE, *Hedyphagetica*.
PAUL WEST,
Words for a Deaf Daughter & Gala.
CURTIS WHITE,
America's Magic Mountain.
The Idea of Home.
Memories of My Father Watching TV.
Monstrous Possibility: An Invitation to Literary Politics.
Requiem.
DIANE WILLIAMS, *Excitability: Selected Stories*.
Romancer Erector.
DOUGLAS WOOLF, *Wall to Wall*.
Ya! & John-Juan.
JAY WRIGHT, *Polynomials and Pollen*.
The Presentable Art of Reading Absence.
PHILIP WYLIE, *Generation of Vipers*.
MARGUERITE YOUNG,
Angel in the Forest.
Miss MacIntosh, My Darling.
REYOUNG, *Unbabbling*.
VLADO ŽABOT, *The Succubus*.
ZORAN ŽIVKOVIĆ, *Hidden Camera*.
LOUIS ZUKOFSKY, *Collected Fiction*.
SCOTT ZWIREN, *God Head*.

FOR A FULL LIST OF PUBLICATIONS, VISIT:
www.dalkeyarchive.com